Have ANNA HIBISCUS!

by Atinuke

illustrated by Lauren Tobia

WALKER
BOOKS

First published 2010 by Walker Books Ltd
87 Vauxhall Walk, London SE11 5HJ

2 4 6 8 10 9 7 5 3

This book has been typeset in StempelSchneidler and Lauren

Printed and bound in Great Britain
by Clays Ltd, St Ives plc

British Library Cataloguing in Publication Data:
a catalogue record for this book is available from the British Library

ISBN 978-1-4063-1508-0

www.walker.co.uk

To my mother with love
A.

To Peter Tobia,
aka Grandad
L.T.

Anna Goes to Canada

Anna Hibiscus lives in Africa. Amazing Africa. She lives with her grandmother and her grandfather, her mother and her father, her aunties and her uncles, her many, many cousins and her two baby brothers, Double and Trouble. But now Anna Hibiscus is going far overseas.

"Is her suitcase in the car?"
Grandfather asked.

"What about her photo album?" called
Grandmother, hurrying over.

"Anna Hibiscus, are you ready?" shouted
Uncle Tunde, standing by the car.

Anna Hibiscus came out of the house,
holding her mother's hand.

"Do you have the book we wrote your
stories in?" shouted cousin Clarity.

"What about your phone money?" asked
Anna Hibiscus's father.

"Is your camera safe?" asked Uncle Eldest.

Anna Hibiscus nodded and nodded.
She had her photo album and her book
and her phone money and her camera in her
new handbag. And in her suitcase was the
surprise present from her mother and the
beautiful new warm red suit and the empty
pot to bring back snow for Double and
Trouble.

Anna Hibiscus was going to Canada.
Today. Now! She was leaving her entire
family and the big white house for one
whole month.

Grandfather held up his hand. "Anna Hibiscus!" he said loudly. At once everybody was quiet. "Do not forget what I have told you!" Grandfather said.

Anna Hibiscus nodded again. Grandfather had told her many things. "Be good, Anna Hibiscus. And have fun. But remember, do not go near any dogs. People in cold countries allow dogs into their houses. This is because they do not live together with the whole of their family as we do here. Instead they have dogs for company."

"Yes, Grandfather," Anna Hibiscus said seriously.

Grandfather had been telling her the same thing since her tickets to Canada had come. But Anna Hibiscus was sure that he was wrong. Nobody would allow a dog into their house. Dogs lived in packs and ate rubbish and bit people. They were thin and angry and had worms.

"Granny Canada will look after you," Grandfather concluded hopefully. "She will not allow you to enter any house which contains a dog. Of that I am sure."

Anna Hibiscus's mother looked as though she was about to say something. Then Double and Trouble started to cry.

Quickly Anna's father put Anna into Uncle
Tunde's car. Her mother jumped in beside
her. But too late. Everybody had
joined Double Trouble in
crying. Chocolate and
Angel were the first.
Then the aunties
started loudly. It
was so sad to say
goodbye.

"Go! Go!" said
Grandmother,
dabbing her eyes.

Uncle Tunde
started the engine.

"Goodbye, Anna!"
sobbed Chocolate
and Angel.

"Don't forget us!"
wailed Benz and
Wonderful.

"Enjoy yourself!" called Thank God and
Sociable.

"Write about everything!" wept
Clarity and Joy and
Common Sense.

"Be careful!" sniffed
Aunty Joly.

"Don't forget to snap
many photos!" called Uncle
Eldest and Uncle Habibi.

"Come back soon!"
sobbed Grandmother and
Grandfather.

"Come soon! Come
soon!" wailed Double
and Trouble.

And they were off.

Anna Hibiscus turned around in her seat to wave. The gates closed behind them. The big white house where Anna Hibiscus had lived all her life was gone.

They turned the corner. The white walls around the garden were gone too.

A big lump came into Anna Hibiscus's throat.

Anna's mother put her arm around her. "Don't worry, Anna," she whispered.

But Anna did worry. She worried all the way to the airport.

The airport was big. Big enough for
aeroplanes to land inside. There were many,
many people running around like ants who
had lost their way.

But Anna Hibiscus's father
knew exactly where to go. He
held Anna's suitcase and headed
across the enormous floor
in one purposeful direction.
Maybe it was the suitcase
that knew what to do. It had
waited so many years to travel.
Now it was eager and ready to go. And
Uncle Tunde and Anna's mother and Anna
Hibiscus all followed.

Anna Hibiscus's father stopped at a little open office. A lady checked the things he gave her. Passport. Ticket.

"They are all correct," she said. "Now, who else is travelling?"

"Just Anna Hibiscus," said her father.

The lady looked at Anna Hibiscus. Then she said, "She is too small. Too small to go alone."

Just then a voice from behind them shouted, *"Femi! Tunde! Emily!* What are you all doing here?"

They all turned around. A big lady was standing there smiling at them. "Auntie Jumoke!" shouted Anna's father and threw his arms around the big lady.

Anna Hibiscus's mother bent her knee to the auntie, who shook her hand warmly.

"Auntie Jum-Jum!" laughed Uncle Tunde. "What are you doing here?"

"I am travelling," said the big auntie. "Aren't I always travelling?" She sighed and shook her head. "Ten children and thirty-four grandchildren and all of them scattered around the world."

17

She looked down at Anna Hibiscus. Then she looked up at Anna Hibiscus's mother and father. "Is this Anna Hibiscus, who gives clothes to poor children?"

Anna Hibiscus's mother and father nodded.

"She is on her way to Canada to visit my mother," said Anna's mother.

"You are like me," sighed the auntie, patting Anna's head. "Family scattered all over the world."

The lady in the office interrupted. "Is this child travelling alone?" she asked again loud and cross.

"Of course not!" replied the big auntie. "We are going together!"

And she said to the lady in the office,
"This is my second cousin's granddaughter."
Which was true.

The big auntie, Auntie Jumoke, arranged
for her seat on the aeroplane to be next
to Anna Hibiscus's seat and together they
watched their suitcases disappear.

Then Anna Hibiscus kissed and hugged
her mother and her father and Uncle Tunde,
and her mother and father again, and her
mother again. Then she started to cry.

"Come here, poor child," said Auntie Jumoke, picking up Anna Hibiscus along with her own seven items of hand luggage. "Before you can say hello to them again, you must first say goodbye."

Then the big auntie, with Anna Hibiscus in her arms, walked around the corner towards the aeroplane, where only the passengers could go.

"Have fun, Anna Hibiscus!" shouted Uncle Tunde.

When they were seated on the plane Auntie Jumoke showed Anna Hibiscus how to fasten her seat belt. She gave her advice on the toilets.

"Only go when it is pressing," she said. "It is not a place you want to visit too often. But do not wait until it is *too* late because there is often a queue. People are so slow!"

Then the plane took off. It carried Anna Hibiscus away from Africa and the beautiful city and her whole family.

Anna Hibiscus held her handbag tight to stop herself from being frightened. Her hands closed around something square and hard. The photo album that Grandmother had made for her!

Anna opened
the photo album
and started to cry.
She wanted to
see her family.
She wanted
to go home.

Auntie Jumoke leaned over
her shoulder. She pointed at a
photo of Anna Hibiscus's father.

"That boy," she sighed. "I
remember one day I asked him
to catch my young cockerel.
He chased it up and down the
compound, up and down.
Eventually the cockerel flew
up onto my roof. Your father
followed him up there. The cockerel flew
down. Your father could not. He had to
remain there until we sent someone to the
next village to borrow a ladder."

22

Anna Hibiscus stopped crying and started to laugh. Before she stopped laughing Auntie Jumoke told her another story. This time about Auntie Joly.

"I sent that girl to the river to wash clothes one day. At her own house she was used to washing at the tap. She scrubbed the clothes on a rock, but when it came time to rinse, she tipped the whole bucket of clothes into the water. The river carried the clothes away and your auntie started to scream and cry. At last a fisherman caught them in his nets and brought them back to me."

Anna Hibiscus could not stop laughing at all the silly things her father and aunties and her uncles and even Grandmother and Grandfather used to do.

Anna Hibiscus laughed all the way across Africa. A lady came along with trays of food. Anna Hibiscus's stomach rumbled. But Auntie Jumoke waved the trays away.

"That is not food," Auntie Jumoke said. "It is plastic, pretending to be food. Only oyinbos from foreign countries can digest that sort of thing."

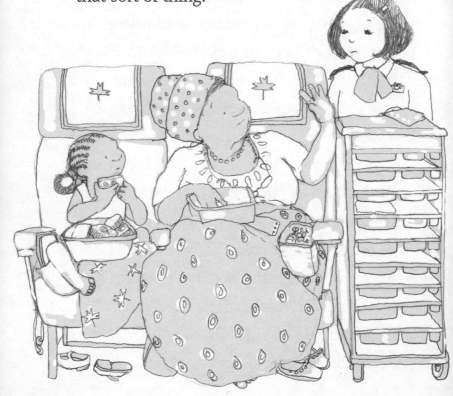

Anna was worried again. Last night she had eaten as much of Uncle Bizi Sunday's good African food as she could squeeze into her belly. She had been sure that she would not be hungry again for a whole month and that she would not have to eat oyinbo food. But she was hungry again already!

Auntie Jumoke was looking in her hand luggage. She pulled out old ice-cream boxes filled with fried chicken and jollof rice and moi-moi.

"Wa jeun!" she said. "Let's eat!"

Suddenly Anna Hibiscus remembered the packets of food that Uncle Bizi Sunday had packed in her suitcase for her. She would not have to eat oyinbo food after all.

Anna Hibiscus smiled happily and shared Auntie Jumoke's food. She ate and ate and ate. Then she fell asleep.

When she woke up the plane was landing in Canada.

Anna Hibiscus stepped out.
It was *so* cold. For a moment
Anna Hibiscus's lungs forgot
how to breathe!

Anna's eyes opened wide.
But there was nothing to see!
The cold had sucked all the
colour out of Canada. Just as it
had sucked the breath out of Anna.
Canada was only white and grey.

Anna Hibiscus followed Auntie Jumoke
through passport control. Then Auntie
Jumoke showed Anna where to find her
suitcase. They walked to where Granny
Canada and all the other passengers' friends
and relatives would be waiting.

Auntie Jumoke was swallowed up by her
own family and Anna Hibiscus stood alone
in front of a sea of white faces. She had
never imagined that there were so many
white faces in the world.

A soft voice said,
"Hello, Anna Hibiscus."

Anna Hibiscus looked up. An old lady who looked just like Granny Canada in her photo stood there.

She put her arms around Anna Hibiscus. And her neck smelled like Anna's mother's neck! Exactly the same! "Hello, Granny Canada," Anna Hibiscus said.

"Hello, Anna Hibiscus," said Granny Canada. "I am glad you are here at last!"

Anna Hibiscus looked down. She wanted to say she was glad too but she was thinking of dogs and plastic food and cold that sucks away breath. She was thinking of her whole family and the big white house so far away. So she said nothing.

28

"Are you ready to see snow?" Granny
Canada asked gently.

Anna Hibiscus nodded. But she still
looked down.

Granny Canada took a big warm red coat
out of her bag. She put it on Anna Hibiscus.
It was just Anna's size. Anna looked
surprised. Then she put a warm fluffy pink
hat on Anna. Then she knelt down and
took off Anna's sandals and put big furry
boots onto her feet.
They fitted perfectly.
She slipped soft pink
gloves onto Anna's
hands. Anna
Hibiscus smiled
at Granny Canada.
She was so surprised. And warm.

Then Granny Canada took Anna's
suitcase and Anna Hibiscus followed her out
of the airport.

The snow was falling thick and white
and bright. The night sky was black.
The moon shone on each flake. Anna
Hibiscus looked up. Her eyes shone
and her mouth opened wide.

"Isn't it lovely?" Granny
Canada asked.

Snowflakes landed on Anna
Hibiscus's face. Anna Hibiscus
nodded. It was lovely. A snowflake
landed on her nose. Anna Hibiscus
laughed. Then she knew. She
was glad to be here too.

Anna Hibiscus started to sing.
First her heart and then her mouth
joined in.

Snow, you are so wonderful,
I am glad to tell you so.
Snow, you are so sweet-o,
I am glad to taste you-o.
Snow, you are wonderful,
I am glad to see you so!

Anna's First Day

Anna Hibiscus is in Canada. Africa, amazing Africa, is very far away. Canada, cold Canada, is where she is now. It is her first day.

Anna Hibiscus woke up. The sheet covering her was so heavy. Where am I? she thought.

There was something warm in her arms.

Anna Hibiscus squeezed it. It was soft. She remembered a hot-water bottle covered with knitted hibiscus flowers. A surprise from her mother.

Her nose was cold. And suddenly Anna Hibiscus remembered where she was! Canada!

Anna jumped straight out of bed. She ran across the cold floor and looked out of the window.

Snow! Snow! Nothing but snow!
Anna Hibiscus sighed happily.

She turned around to tell
her cousins. But there was
nobody there.
Only an empty
bed piled high
with blankets
and duvets
and a lonely pink
hot-water bottle.
Anna Hibiscus was alone. For the first
time in her life, she had woken up alone.

There was a knock on the door. Anna Hibiscus rushed to open it. It was Granny Canada. And a dog. A big white dog with sharp pointed teeth who jumped into the room.

Anna Hibiscus closed her eyes and screamed.

"Qimmiq!" said Granny Canada's voice. "Down! Out!"

Anna Hibiscus heard the door shut. The dog was gone.

"Anna?" said Granny Canada's soft voice. "I'm sorry. I did not know that you were afraid of dogs."

38

Anna Hibiscus did not say anything. Everybody was afraid of dogs.

"Her name is Qimmiq," said Granny Canada. "I have had her all her life and she has never, ever hurt anybody."

Anna Hibiscus still said nothing. Dogs had worms and germs and they liked to bite people.

"Anna Hibiscus," said Granny Canada, "Qimmiq only wants to be your friend."

Anna Hibiscus could never be friends with a dog. Anna Hibiscus's heart made a miserable noise.

From behind the door came exactly the same noise. Anna opened her eyes in surprise.

"It is Qimmiq," said Granny Canada. "She is miserable. She does not understand why she is shut out alone."

Anna Hibiscus was so surprised. She kept her eyes open wide.

"Let us unpack your suitcase and get you dressed," said Granny Canada. "You must be cold."

So Anna Hibiscus unpacked socks and pants and vests and her two long-sleeved dresses. Then she watched in surprise as Granny Canada opened drawers and brought out long yellow socks that went right up and turned into knickers.

"Tights," said Granny Canada.

Granny Canada also brought out a yellow long-sleeved t-shirt and a thick blue long-sleeved t-shirt and a knitted cardigan and thick padded blue trousers.

Anna Hibiscus looked at the pile of clothes. Was she supposed to wear all of those? At once! "Come on," said Granny Canada.

So Anna Hibiscus put on her pants and her vest. What was supposed to go on next? Granny Canada passed Anna Hibiscus the

long-sleeved t-shirt. Anna
pulled it on.

Granny Canada held out
the tights. Anna Hibiscus
looked at them. She had never
worn anything like them before.

"This way round," Granny
Canada said.

Anna Hibiscus
sat on the bed
and put one of
her feet slowly into
the tights.

"That's it," said
Granny Canada.

"Slowly, or the legs will get twisted."
Anna Hibiscus's foot got stuck. She
pushed it. But the tights would not let her
foot go in any further. Granny Canada bent
over and pulled the tights out straight.

"Try now," she said.

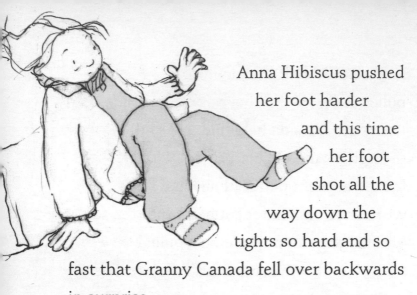

Anna Hibiscus pushed
her foot harder
and this time
her foot
shot all the
way down the
tights so hard and so
fast that Granny Canada fell over backwards
in surprise.

Anna Hibiscus jumped up to help Granny
Canada. But she forgot that she had only
had one foot in the tights. Anna Hibiscus fell
down next to Granny Canada.

Granny Canada laughed and laughed.
She could not stop. Anna Hibiscus
started to laugh too.

At last Granny Canada took a handkerchief out of her pocket and wiped her eyes. "Let's start again," she said.

She took the tangled leg of the tights and bunched it up open so that Anna Hibiscus could fit her other foot straight into the foot of the tights. Granny Canada pulled the tights all the way up Anna Hibiscus's legs to her waist.

"I think it is safe to get up now," she said.

Anna Hibiscus got up. She looked down at her legs. They were yellow. They were so yellow that they did a little yellow dance. Anna Hibiscus was surprised. She did not know that her legs would like being yellow so much.

Granny Canada smiled. She passed Anna Hibiscus the rest of the clothes and after a lot of wriggling and pushing and straightening and pulling, Anna Hibiscus was in!

"Breakfast?" asked Granny Canada.

Anna Hibiscus's stomach rumbled in reply.

"Coming?" asked Granny Canada with her hand on the door.

Anna Hibiscus did not answer. She did not move. Then she said, "Dogs have germs and they like to bite people."

"Not all dogs," said Granny Canada. "Have you ever been bitten by a dog?"

Anna Hibiscus shook her head.

"I have never been near to a dog to let it bite me," she said.

"You have never been near a dog?" asked Granny Canada in surprise.

Anna Hibiscus shook her head.

"Never stroked a dog?"

Anna Hibiscus shook her head hard.

"Don't you have friends who have dogs?" asked Granny Canada.

"No," said Anna Hibiscus. "Dogs live outside and eat rubbish. They are dirty.

People chase them away so that they don't bite children or bring sickness."

"Oh," said Granny Canada.

Granny Canada went out and shut the dog in another room. Then Anna Hibiscus came out and followed Granny Canada to the kitchen.

Anna Hibiscus looked round the room in surprise. There were cupboards and a sink and a fridge, and there was also a sofa and arm chairs and a table in the middle. It was not just a kitchen! It was a kitchen-living-dining room. Anna had never seen one of these before!

Granny Canada opened cupboards and started putting packets on the table. Anna Hibiscus remembered what Auntie Jumoke had said about plastic food.

Anna Hibiscus ran down the corridor and back to her own room. When Granny Canada turned around, Anna Hibiscus was sitting at the table surrounded by packets of red spicy-looking food.

"That looks good," said Granny Canada. "Shall I put the chocolate cereal away?"

Chocolate cereal! Anna Hibiscus's eyes opened wide. Once Auntie Comfort had brought cereal from America for the cousins. But not chocolate cereal!

Anna Hibiscus looked at Uncle Bizi Sunday's packets. She could eat them anytime. She could eat them for lunch!

"Chocolate cereal for breakfast, I think!" Anna Hibiscus said.

She wished that her cousins were here to share this. Anna could not wait to phone and tell them all about it.

Thinking about her cousins made her feel sad. But she could not phone now. They would still be asleep.

So after breakfast, to cheer herself up,
Anna Hibiscus read to Granny Canada from
the book where her cousins had written
down all her adventures. Granny Canada
loved the bit where Anna sold oranges on
the street. She loved the bit where
Double and Trouble ate all
the sweets.

Anna Hibiscus showed Granny Canada
the photos in her album of everybody in her
stories. That made her feel sad again. A tear
dripped off Anna's nose. Then the dog barked.

"You are missing them," said Granny
Canada. "And Qimmiq is missing me."

Anna Hibiscus was so surprised she
stopped crying.

Granny Canada took down her big photo album and showed Anna the photos.

"Who is this in the snow?" Anna Hibiscus asked, pointing at a brown photograph of a small man surrounded by snow.

"That is your great-great-grandfather," said Granny Canada. "His smile reminds me of someone..."

"My great-great-grandfather?" said Anna Hibiscus. She had forgotten that Granny Canada's family was her family too.

"Yes," said Granny Canada. "He lived out on the snow and the ice all his life."

Wow! thought Anna Hibiscus. Maybe that was why she loved snow so much. Because she had a snow family too.

"He loved snow," said Granny Canada. "But one day he almost died out on the ice."

"How did he almost die?" asked Anna Hibiscus.

"He was hunting a seal when he fell through the ice and into the frozen sea."

"What happened?" asked Anna Hibiscus.

Granny Canada smiled. "Luckily someone else was there and he was rescued."

"How?" asked Anna.

"He was pulled out of the hole in the ice," said Granny Canada. "Someone risked their own life to save him."

"Who?" gasped Anna Hibiscus.

"His favourite dog," said Granny Canada.

"His dog!" Anna Hibiscus was shocked.

"Oh yes," said Granny Canada. "He had many dogs. They pulled his sledge and helped him hunt food. Our family could not have survived out on the snow without dogs. And this one saved him from certain death."

"From certain death!" gasped Anna Hibiscus.

Granny Canada pointed to a photo of a big white dog with white pointed teeth.

"If the first Qimmiq had not saved your grandfather, I would not have been born," said Granny Canada. "Nor would your mother."

"Oh," said Anna Hibiscus. Then she thought, Nor me. I would not have been born either.

Granny Canada said, "Time for a walk. Let us go and see the snow we love. Qimmiq must come. She needs exercise."

So Anna Hibiscus and Granny Canada
and Qimmiq went for a walk in the snow.
Granny Canada kept Quimmiq on a strong
lead. Anna Hibiscus stayed well away from
her big teeth. But she looked at her out of
the corner of her eye.

"She is the many times granddaughter of
the first Qimmiq," said Granny Canada.

"Oh!" said Anna Hibiscus again. Then she
stopped looking at Qimmiq and looked at
the snow instead.

Heaps of snow! Banks of snow! Fields of
snow!

Out of a snowdrift a chimney was pouring
smoke. Anna Hibiscus laughed out loud.

That was not a snowdrift!
That was a house!

Anna Hibiscus took photos of the snow
with the camera her uncles had given her.
She took lots of the snowdrift chimney
and laughed again.

Then Granny Canada took
photos of Anna in the snow.
Anna ran across the snow.
It was crunchy and hard.
She made snowballs.
She and Granny
Canada made
snow angels.
They made
a snowman.

"Time to go in now, Anna Hibiscus," said Granny Canada. But Anna Hibiscus was running on the snow, listening to the *crunch, crunch, crunch*. She wanted to run for ever across the bright and shiny snow and never stop.

"Come on, Anna," called Granny Canada, "before you get too cold!"

But Anna Hibiscus did not hear. She was climbing up a snowdrift now.

Suddenly Anna Hibiscus disappeared headfirst into the snowdrift.

"Anna!" shouted Granny Canada and let go of Qimmiq's lead.

Deep in the snowdrift Anna Hibiscus struggled. The more she moved, the deeper she fell. The snow was heavy on her arms and legs and on the back of her head. Anna Hibiscus could not breathe.

I am going to die, she thought.

Somebody caught hold of Anna Hibiscus's foot and pulled hard. They pulled her out of the snowdrift and up into the air. Anna Hibiscus lay on the ground and breathed. The air was cold but it was so lovely to breathe.

Anna Hibiscus looked up. There was nobody there. Nobody except Qimmiq. She was sitting quietly with her head on one side looking at Anna with worried eyes.

Granny Canada arrived running and caught Anna Hibiscus up in her arms and hugged her.

"Are you OK? " Granny asked.

"She saved me! She saved me!" Anna Hibiscus cried. "Just like Great-Great-Grandfather! She saved me from certain death!"

Anna Hibiscus stopped hugging Granny Canada. She looked at Qimmiq and smiled. Then she very carefully stroked the big white dog.

"Thank you for saving me," Anna Hibiscus said. Then she smiled and she smiled.

And suddenly Granny Canada realized exactly who Great-Great-Grandfather's smile reminded her of.

Why, Anna Hibiscus, of course!

Cousins or Friends?

Anna Hibiscus is in Canada. Cold, cold
Canada. Africa, amazing Africa, is far, far
away. But Canada is amazing too.

Anna Hibiscus was sitting in Granny
Canada's kitchen-living-dining room.
Qimmiq was warm and heavy on her feet.
Hot chocolate was steaming under her nose.
Granny Canada's knitting needles were
clack-clack-clacking happily. Anna Hibiscus
was writing in her "Adventures of Anna
Hibiscus" book. The one her cousins had
made for her.

Canada is full of ice and snow. Ice is cold. Snow is cold. Especially when I fell all the way into it. But Canada is COSY too. Cosy means warm and safe and happy. Granny Canada's kitchen is cosy. Good dogs like Qimmiq are cosy.

Anna was writing. And thinking ... that there was one big C word that Canada was not. And that was Cousins. Canada did not mean cousins.

Anna Hibiscus missed her cousins. She could not stop missing them.

Anna wanted Benz and Wonderful to eat chocolate cereal with her every single morning. She wanted to jump into her big hot baths with Chocolate and Angel. Anna wanted Clarity and Joy and Common Sense to walk with around the big bright shiny shops that sold every single thing in the world!

 She wanted Miracle and Sweetheart to hear all the new stories that Granny Canada knew.

Suddenly
Anna Hibiscus
stopped writing
and thinking.

She had heard something. Something
outside. Anna Hibiscus ran to the window.

"Look! Look! Look!" she shouted.

Qimmiq jumped up at the window. She
wagged her tail fast.

Children had stopped outside Granny
Canada's gate. They looked like they were
going somewhere, carrying big bright plastic
bowls and boards.

Quick, quick! Anna Hibiscus fought her
way into her snowsuit and her hat and her
gloves.

Anna Hibiscus rushed out into Granny
Canada's yard with Qimmiq barking beside
her.

"Hello!" Anna
Hibiscus shouted.

All the children
turned to look at Anna Hibiscus.

One boy said, "We were thinking of
ringing your bell."

A big girl with freckles said, "Do you want
to play?"

"Oh yes!" said Anna Hibiscus. She was so
happy.

Anna looked up at the house. Granny
Canada was waving. "Go and play!" she
shouted, smiling.

"Cool!" said the big girl.

"Cool!" said the big boy.

"Cool?" asked Anna Hibiscus.

"Come on!" shouted all the children.

The children started to run down the road, laughing and carrying their big plastic bowls and boards.

Anna Hibiscus and Qimmiq followed, Qimmiq's head bumping on Anna's hand.

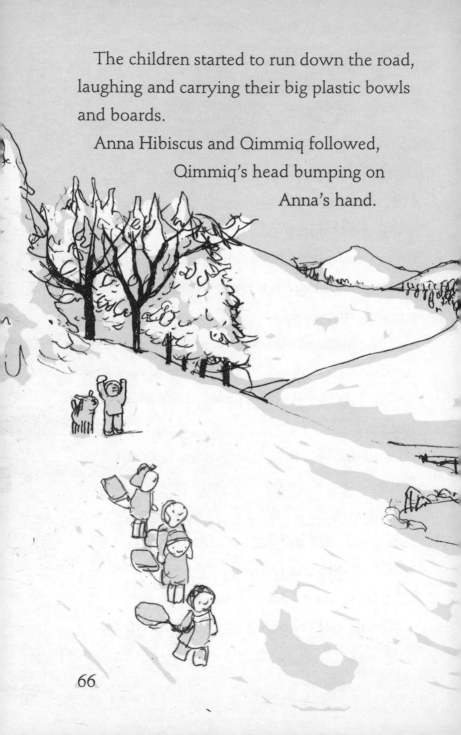

They ran out of the town to a steep
bumpy slope and a frozen lake. There was
not one single footprint in the shining white
snow. The lake was smooth. The trees all
around it dangled sparkling icicles. The
mountains rose up behind them, strong
and watchful. And some ravens were
there too, black against the blue sky,
waving their long feathers.

Anna Hibiscus took
a deep happy breath.

She watched the other children drop their boards and bowls and run shouting and shrieking down the slope to the lake. Anna Hibiscus followed. At the bottom, one of the girls gave Anna Hibiscus some boots. The boots had metal on the bottom. Anna Hibiscus recognized them. Skates!

This lake must be safe for skating on!

"I brought them for you," said the girl shyly. "They used to be mine. Will you be my friend? I never had a friend from Africa before."

Anna Hibiscus did not know whether to say yes or no. Did the girl want to be her friend only because she was from Africa? So Anna just put on the skates. She had seen so many photographs of her mother skating. Anna Hibiscus wanted to skate too. It looked just like flying!

Anna Hibiscus stood up on the ice and fell
down on her face. Ow! Everybody laughed!

The girl who wanted to be her friend tried
to pull her up, but Anna slipped again and
pulled the girl over with her. Ow! Ow!

The other children laughed even harder.

The girl got up and skated away.

She did not want to be

laughed at too.

Anna watched her go. So that girl
did not really want to be Anna's friend after
all. But Anna Hibiscus was not going to give
up. She could learn to skate on her own.

A cross-looking boy skated close to Anna.

"You can't skate because you are African," he said.

Anna Hibiscus sat down on the ice with a thump. She wanted to shout but there was a big hard lump in her throat. She took off the skates. She wanted to go back to Granny Canada's. But she did not know how to get there.

The other children skated for a long time. When they were finished Anna followed them back up the slope towards the town. They were all talking to each other and laughing. Nobody spoke to her. Anna Hibiscus was glad to be going home.

But when the
children got to the
top of the slope, they
picked up the bowls
and boards they had left
there and turned to face
the lake again.

One by one and two by
two they got onto their boards
and slid down the snowy
slope. Faster and faster they
went – until they hit a big bump
in the snow and the plastic slides
bounced up and everybody fell off.

Nobody reached the bottom.
Anna Hibiscus and Qimmiq
watched and watched.
Anna could not take
her eyes off the
snow slides. She
forgot everything else.

71

"Do you want to have a go?" a small voice asked. It was the same girl who had lent Anna her old skates. Now she was holding out her snow slide.

"Yes," said Anna, without taking her eyes off the snow.

She took the snow slide. She looked down the slope. Anna Hibiscus got onto the slide.

"Does anyone want to take her down?" called the big girl with freckles.

But nobody did. They had all seen how badly Anna Hibiscus skated. Who would want to go on a snow slide with her?

Anna Hibiscus was glad. She wanted to be alone, skimming down the slope. Unless…

Anna Hibiscus looked at Qimmiq. Qimmiq jumped onto the slide with Anna. The children laughed. Anna Hibiscus did not care.

She was off!
Anna Hibiscus
could hear the snow
crunch under her slide.
Somehow she knew
which way
to lean over every
bump so that she
soared through the
air. She was flying!
Anna Hibiscus flew
all the way down to
the bottom of the
slope without
falling off once!

At the bottom Anna
Hibiscus laughed.
Qimmiq rolled
around in
the snow,
barking.

73

Then Anna Hibiscus heard shouting.
All the children were running and shrieking
down the slope towards her.

Anna Hibiscus watched them. She did not
smile.

"That was so cool!" yelled the boys.

"So cool!" they all shouted.

"How did you do that?" asked the big girl.

The cross boy was the last one to arrive.
"Africans can't do that!" he shouted.

Anna Hibiscus wished that Grandmother
was here to say a thing or
two to that boy. But she was
in Africa. Anna Hibiscus
was alone. And she knew
that if she did not say
something now,
she would feel
ashamed.

So Anna Hibiscus looked
the children in the eye.

"My name is Anna Hibiscus," said Anna. "I could not skate because it was my first time. Not because I am African."

The cross boy's face went red and he looked at the ground.

Anna said, "I don't know why I am good at snow sliding. I just am. Because I am Anna."

One of the girls looked like she was going to say something.

But Anna said quickly, "I only want to be friends with people who want to be friends with me because I am Anna. Not because I am African."

Then Anna Hibiscus stopped talking. Her throat felt dry.

Some of the other children were looking at her and some were looking down at the snow. None of them said anything now.

Anna started to
trudge up the slope
alone with Qimmiq. She
was going to go back
now. Even if she got lost.
Before she got to the
top a voice shouted, "Stop!"
Anna Hibiscus turned
around. The children were
following her up.

"We are sorry, Anna
Hibiscus," said one of the
big girls.

"Really sorry," said one
of the little boys.

"We did not know
it was your first time
skating," said another
girl. "Honestly."

Anna Hibiscus took
a deep breath.

76

"OK," she said.

"How come it was your first time?" asked the little girl. "What do you do in the winter in Africa?"

"We don't have winter in Africa," said Anna Hibiscus.

"No winter!" the cross boy shouted. "No snow? No ice? Not at all?"

Anna Hibiscus shook her head.

"So, what do you have?" he asked.

"We have the harmattan," said Anna Hibiscus, "and the rainy season."

"What's that?" asked a girl.

Anna Hibiscus explained about the harmattan wind blowing sand from the Sahara Desert all the way across Africa. And she explained about the rainy season, when it rains for six months and the roads flood and turn to mud.

"Cool!" said one of the girls.

"Wow!" said a big boy.

Anna Hibiscus
stopped talking. She did not
tell them about the big white house
or about Grandmother and Grandfather
and her cousins and the mango trees and
the chickens. She did not tell them about
Double and Trouble, her brothers.

She did not know if she liked them yet.

Then one of the big boys said, "Do you
want to use my snow slide, Anna Hibiscus?"

"Go on, Anna," said one of the big girls.
"His board has never made it all the way
down before."

"Yeah," said another boy. "You'd be doing
it a favour!"

Anna Hibiscus smiled. She took the big
board the boy was holding out. Anna and
Qimmiq got on.

78

There was room for more
children. Anna Hibiscus looked
over her shoulder. "Taxi!" she shouted.
The children laughed. Two of them
jumped on.

"I'm Lauren!" shouted
one of them.

"I'm Cara!"
shouted the other.
And off they
flew!

Anna Hibiscus spent the rest of the day
flying down the slope with Cara and Lauren
and Tessa and Rosie and Tom and Steve and
Joe and Mark.

"I was wrong, Anna Hibiscus," said Tom,
the cross boy, as they walked home.

"Africans are cool."

Soon they were at Granny Canada's gate.

"See you tomorrow!" everybody shouted.

"We'll come and get you," said Cara.

"We'll bring our slides," said Tom.

"And our skates!" said Lauren.

Everybody laughed.

"Do you *want* to play with us again tomorrow?" Rosie asked.

"Yes!" said Anna Hibiscus. "Definitely."

"Cool!" shouted all the children.

"Canada is so cool!" Anna Hibiscus told Grandfather that night on the phone.

"Don't you mean cold?" His voice crackled.

"Let me hear her," Anna heard Grandmother's voice say.

"Canada is cool," Anna told Grandmother.

"She means cold," Grandmother's voice said to Grandfather.

"There are no cousins here," Anna told Angel and Clarity and Benz.

"But I have got friends," she told her mother.

"Friends?" asked Double.

"Friends!" said Anna Hibiscus. "They are not so kind as cousins. Not so brilliant as brothers. But they are cool. Friends are definitely cool!"

Anna's Christmas in Canada

Anna Hibiscus is in Canada. Cold, cosy, cool Canada!

It was Christmas Eve. Anna Hibiscus was in the kitchen-living-dining room with Granny Canada. She had been there for days. Mixing butter and sugar. Sifting flour and baking powder. Beating eggs and cream. Measuring cinnamon and nutmeg and ginger. Stirring in cherries and raisins and currants. Melting chocolate and molasses.

Can you guess what she was making?

Sweet pastries and mince
pies, rich fruitcakes and chocolate
yule-logs, pumpkin pies and trifle,
eggnog and gingerbread houses.
Christmas food, of course!

Anna Hibiscus had never tasted
Canadian Christmas food before.
She had heard about it from her
mother. She had wondered
what it tasted like.
Now she knew.
It tasted like heaven.
Sweet and creamy
and rich and …
heavenly!
Anna Hibiscus
stopped stirring and mixing
and beating for a second.

At home in the big white compound in Africa, the goats and chickens would be fattening.

Uncle Bizi Sunday would be frying a mountain of rice and crayfish. Bean curd moi-moi wrapped in plantain leaves would be boiling in oil drums.

Aunties would be pounding, pounding, pounding creamy yams. Anna Hibiscus's mouth was watering.

Canada's Christmas food tasted like heaven. It was true. But African Christmas food was the best food on earth! Spicy and savoury and mouth-watering...

Granny Canada looked at Anna Hibiscus. "Excited about tonight?" she guessed.

Anna Hibiscus nodded. She was very excited. Tonight she was going carol singing in the snow for the very first time!

"But first," said Granny Canada, "the Christmas tree!"

Anna Hibiscus ran to the sink to wash her hands and hang up her apron. Granny Canada brought out the big box of Christmas decorations. Decorations that were already old when Granny Canada was a girl.

Anna Hibiscus was amazed to see tiny candle-holders and carved wooden reindeer. There were baubles made of coloured glass. And snowflakes baked with cinnamon and painted with glue to make them shiny. Anna Hibiscus and Granny Canada hung them all carefully on the tree.

Last of all was the Christmas angel.
Granny Canada held tight to the long ladder
and Anna Hibiscus climbed to the top. Anna
Hibiscus carefully tied the angel to the top
of the tree with the ribbons behind her big
golden wings.

Then Granny Canada and Anna Hibiscus
stood back and looked at the beautiful
glittering sweet-smelling tree.
It was the most
beautiful tree
Anna had
ever seen.

Anna Hibiscus thought again about her family at home in Africa.

They too would be busy in the compound of the big white house. Her big boy cousins would be up ladders, covering every tree and bush and window and balcony in the compound with glittering, twinkling fairy lights. The whole compound would become magical. And loud with Christmas carols played from every radio around.

Anna looked out of the window again.
Granny Canada's yard was decorated in
bright silent snow.

Anna Hibiscus sighed happily. It was
lovely here. And it was wonderful there.
Now she was here. But soon she would be
back there. Everything was perfect.

"Time to get ready!" Granny Canada said.

Anna Hibiscus ran to put on her most beautiful clothes, ready for the carol singing. She chose the red suit that her African aunties had made especially to keep out the Canada cold. It had a full skirt that twirled when she turned around and a jacket and even a little hat to match.

"You look gorgeous," said Granny Canada. "All red like the winter berries in the snow."

And she lit a candle lantern and took Anna Hibiscus outside, where the candlelight shone out and danced on the snow.

Anna looked down at herself. In Africa she was red like the hibiscus flower, like her name. Here she was red like winter berries in the snow. Anna Hibiscus sighed happily. Again everything was perfect.

Granny Canada took photographs of red-berry Anna all lit up by candlelight and smiling her great-great-grandfather smile. Granny Canada had to wipe her eyes. Maybe because it was so cold.

"*Ding dong merrily on high!*" rang out voices in the street.

"*In heaven the bells are ringing!*" Anna Hibiscus joined in loudly.

"Hello, Anna Hibiscus," called Cara and Rosie and Joe.

93

From street to street and house to house
they sang. "Away in a Manger", "Mary's
Boy Child" and "Silent Night", all the carols
that Anna Hibiscus knew already. And new
ones, like "Jingle Bells" and "Once in Royal
David's City" and "Chestnuts Roasting on
an Open Fire" that she had just learnt.

One door was opened by a smiling
woman. Anna
Hibiscus peeped
past into her
pretty house.
At that same
moment a girl
peeped around
from behind
the woman to
see the carol
singers!

Anna Hibiscus was so surprised that she stopped singing. The other girl had very curly black hair just like Anna's, and skin the same colour as Anna's! She looked just as surprised as Anna Hibiscus did.

Before Anna could say anything, the carol singers started to walk on.

"Glad tidings we bring, to you and your kin," they sang.

Anna Hibiscus kept looking over her shoulder at the smiling woman and the surprised girl until they were gone.

Christmas morning Anna Hibiscus woke up early. Snow was falling thickly but Anna was warm in her bed. Cuddled in her arms was the hot-water bottle in its hibiscus flower cover that her mother had knitted for her. And lying over her feet was a warm and heavy snoring shape.

"Qimmiq!" shouted Anna Hibiscus. "It's Christmas!"

Qimmiq stretched up and licked her on the nose!

"Qimmiq!" giggled Anna Hibiscus. "What would Grandfather say!"

It was a good question. Anna Hibiscus did not want to know the answer. What was she going to say to Grandfather about Qimmiq? Anna Hibiscus did not know the answer to that either.

So she jumped out of bed and ran to
the kitchen. There above the fire hung her
stocking, full and lumpy, and under the tree
was a pile of brightly wrapped presents.

Anna shrieked happily. In her stocking
were oranges and nuts and chocolate. Anna
Hibiscus busied herself with eating them
until Granny Canada woke up and made
hot chocolate
and settled
down in front
of the fire.

Then Anna Hibiscus opened her presents.
There were knitting needles and wool
from Granny Canada.

A beautiful red necklace
and earrings to match
her red suit
sent especially
from her family in the
big white house in
Africa. And from Cara
and Lauren and Tessa
and Rosie and

Tom and Steve and Joe
and Mark … a snow
slide of her own!
Anna Hibiscus
clapped her hands
in delight.
"That will have to
live here and wait for your
visits," said Granny Canada.

After eating pancakes with maple syrup,
Anna Hibiscus and Granny Canada
went out to the slope
by the lake.

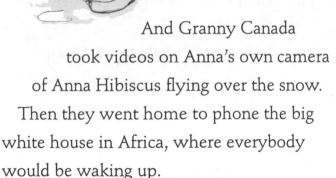

And Granny Canada
took videos on Anna's own camera
of Anna Hibiscus flying over the snow.
Then they went home to phone the big
white house in Africa, where everybody
would be waking up.

Anna Hibiscus had just finished saying, "Merry Christmas! I love you! See you in *two* days!" to everybody when the doorbell rang.

Anna Hibiscus ran to the door. It was the smiling woman and the girl that Anna Hibiscus had seen carol singing! They had come to meet Anna Hibiscus!

"I am Tiger Lily," said the girl shyly.

"And I'm Anna Hibiscus," said Anna. "I'm from Africa."

She waited for Tiger Lily to say that she was from Africa too.

"I'm from Canada," said Tiger Lily.

"Oh, " said Anna.

"But in two days I'm going to Africa," Tiger Lily said.

"Me too!" said Anna excitedly.

Tiger Lily was going to visit her father in Africa on the very same day that Anna was going home.

Then they discovered that Anna Hibiscus's father and Tiger Lily's father lived in the very same African city. Which was amazing because Africa is huge and has fifty-three different countries and zillions of cities.

"But I have never been to Africa before," said Tiger Lily, looking very worried.

Anna looked at Tiger Lily's face. She said, "I had not been to Canada before either. I had not even met Granny Canada before I came."

Tiger Lily looked at Anna Hibiscus sitting happily on Granny Canada's lap. She stopped looking so worried.

* * *

And now it was today. Today that Anna
Hibiscus was leaving Canada and flying back
home to Africa with Tiger Lily and Auntie
Jumoke. They were flying on the same plane.
Auntie Jumoke had arranged it all.

"Time to go!" called Granny Canada.

Anna Hibiscus threw on her coat, grabbed
Double and Trouble's empty jar and ran
outside. At the very last minute she filled it
with snow and packed it into Granny
Canada's summer picnic
cooler to keep the
snow frozen all
the way to Africa.

"Bye, Qimmiq," said Anna Hibiscus.

Quimmiq barked. And Anna Hibiscus put her arms around her neck. "You are my best friend," she whispered. "My very best friend!"

Qimmiq barked softly and Anna Hibiscus burst into tears. All the way to the airport she cried.

There they met Tiger Lily and her mother.
Tiger Lily was crying too.

Auntie Jumoke was waiting for them with
one huge overflowing piece of hand luggage.
She took one look at the two girls and
started to laugh.

"This one," she said, patting Anna
Hibiscus's head, "seems to cry before
boarding a plane no matter which direction
she is headed."

"And this one," said Auntie Jumoke, putting her arm gently around Tiger Lily, "will also be crying when it's time to come back."

Then Auntie Jumoke said to Tiger Lily's mother, "I will personally visit her every day and vouch for her happiness. If she is not happy I will return her immediately, myself."

So Tiger Lily stopped crying and smiled.

Then Granny Canada bought a big Canada sticker from the airport shop and Anna Hibiscus stuck it proudly onto the suitcase that Grandfather had given her.

Granny Canada hugged Anna Hibiscus.

"I love you so much, Anna Hibiscus," Granny Canada said. "Come back soon."

"I love you too Granny Canada," Anna Hibiscus said. "Thank you for telling me all the stories about Great-Great-Grandfather and making hot chocolate and Qimmiq…"

Anna Hibiscus burst into tears.

"Time to go!" said Auntie Jumoke.

107

Auntie Jumoke led them to where only
the passengers could go. She loaded them
onto the plane. She gave them advice about
seat belts and toilets. Then she unpacked
her hand luggage. Jollof rice and moi-moi
and fried fish and yam balls and hot-hot red
spicy stew.

Tiger Lily looked worried.

Anna Hibiscus smiled and opened her bag. She took out the sandwiches and yogurt and crisps that Granny Canada had packed for her.

"Have these," she said, giving them to Tiger Lily.

"Are you sure?" asked Tiger Lily.

"Yes," said Anna Hibiscus. Her stomach growled. She could not wait to eat the jollof rice and moi-moi! And she had chocolate cereal in her suitcase. Enough to last her and her cousins for a whole year.

Auntie Jumoke sighed and shook her head as the girls swapped their food. Tiger Lily smiled.

And Anna Hibiscus –
Anna Hibiscus laughed.

Atinuke was born in Nigeria and spent her childhood in both Africa and the UK. She works as a storyteller in schools and in theatres, telling traditional African tales and reading from her books about Anna Hibiscus, and also the No. 1 Car Spotter. *Have Fun, Anna Hibiscus!* is her fifth book. Atinuke lives with her husband and two young sons in Wales.

Lauren Tobia lives in Southville, Bristol. She shares her tiny house with her husband and their two yappy Jack Russell terriers. When Lauren is not drawing, she can be found drinking tea on her allotment. *Have Fun, Anna Hibiscus!* is her fifth book.